Flying
Bombs

Stories linking with the History
National Curriculum Key Stage 2.

First published in 1998 by Franklin Watts
338 Euston Road, London NW1 3BH

Franklin Watts Australia
Level 17/207 Kent Street, Sydney NSW 2000

This edition published 2002

Editor: Kyla Barber
Designer: Jason Anscomb
Consultant: Dr Anne Millard, BA Hons, Dip Ed, PhD

A CIP catalogue record for this book
is available from the British Library.

ISBN 978 0 7496 4599 1

Dewey Classification 941.043

Printed in Great Britain

Franklin Watts is a division of Hachette Children's Books,
an Hachette Livre UK company.
www.hachettelivre.co.uk

Flying Bombs

by
Dennis Hamley

Illustrations by George Buchanan

W
FRANKLIN WATTS
LONDON•SYDNEY

1

The Coming of the Doodlebugs

One June night in 1944, all seemed quiet and peaceful on the North Downs in Kent. As she lay awake in bed, Josie heard a faraway noise like a motorbike. The noise came nearer. If the bike was climbing the road up the hill, it should be slowing down and changing gear by now. This must be a very powerful motorbike. The noise was deafening. Suddenly scared, Josie tumbled out of bed, lifted the blackout and looked through the window. The noise was not on the road: it was in the sky.

And now there was a terrifying sight above her – a tiny aeroplane, very fast and low. Its black, stubby little wings made it look like a flying cross. Flame poured out of the back as if it had been hit. But surely nothing which flew so fast could be damaged? And the noise! – a rackety roar so loud it seemed the horrible object must shake itself into pieces.

And then it was gone.

The noise died away as it continued
its course dead straight towards London.
Josie got back in bed. What was it? A
German plane which had been hit?
Then why didn't it crash?

Like most other people, she knew
the shape of every aeroplane, allied and
enemy – and this was like nothing she had
ever seen. It was ugly, sinister and, even
though she only saw it for a second or two,
deeply, deeply scary.

Nobody believed her at school.

"You're having us on."

"You dreamt it, Josie."

"You're talking rubbish. No Jerry planes dare show their faces over here any more, not now we're winning." This from Alfie Perkins, whom Josie couldn't stand. "Besides, what do girls know about it?"

More than you think, Josie thought. That evening she listened to the news on the wireless. She waited through reports of how we were chasing the enemy through France and Italy, about the Russians pushing west and the Americans beating the Japanese in the Pacific. Then, at last – "The Air Ministry reports that a single enemy raider was shot down in the London area last night." Was that all? Perhaps it wasn't anything to worry about after all.

That night, everything was quiet. And the next. Two more nights passed: Josie wondered whether it had been a dream.

But, five nights after the first, the noise came again – a huge, badly-tuned motorbike. Once more, Josie looked out of her window. The same ugly black cross was moving fast in the sky, with the same streaming flame, on the way to London. No sooner had its noise died away than another gruff chattering came from the south. Five minutes later came another. And another. And another.

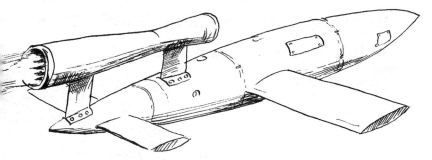

There was crying from the next room. Josie went in to find Mum rocking little David to and fro. "It's all right. Nasty old Mr Hitler can't get you, my sweet."

Overhead at intervals the roaring kept coming. Soon they had lost count.

"Mum, what is it?" cried Josie.

"I wish I knew, love," Mum answered.

So something terrible was happening. The war wasn't over at all.

Next day, everybody knew. The Home Secretary told Parliament of this new threat. The pilotless aircraft. The Flying Bomb. The V1 – "V for Vengeance", said the Germans. Scores had landed all across south London and exploded. It was like the Blitz all over again. That evening an RAF officer was interviewed on the wireless. He called these awful flying bombs "Doodlebugs". The name stuck.

2

Tom

A doodlebug landed in the next street to
Auntie Mabel in London twenty miles away.
The blast blew all the slates off her roof.

"That's it," she said. "We're off!"

There was only one place to go – the
little cottage on top of the North Downs

where Josie, her mother and little brother David lived. Mabel packed all she could and then set off south with her son Tom, Josie's cousin. Their fathers were away at war. Josie's father was on a destroyer in the Atlantic. Tom's Dad, Josie's Uncle Bert, was with the army in France.

Mabel and Tom reached the cottage that evening. "Sorry to barge in," said Auntie Mabel. "But we can't stay in Clapham."

It was all right for Josie and her family. The doodlebugs were aimed at London. So Josie's Mum said, "Of course you can't stay there, Mabel. Make yourselves comfortable here for as long as you like."

Tom scowled at Josie, who thought, *I'm not going to enjoy this very much.*

Tom was a year younger than Josie and they didn't really like each other.

"We must look after our guests properly. Auntie Mabel and Tom will sleep in your room. You can go in the attic," said Mum.

Josie liked Tom even less. She had to climb up a ladder to the attic, a tiny room with a sloping roof and little dormer window. As she lay in the rickety camp bed, listening to Tom complaining in the bedroom below, she felt high up in the sky – far too close to flying doodlebugs.

13

That night their noise seemed even louder, the flames which followed them brighter. She lay still and counted them until she felt dizzy. Counting sheep sent you to sleep. Counting doodlebugs made sure you stayed awake.

Next morning, Josie had to take Tom to school with her. This wasn't pleasant. He never stopped going on about how dangerous it was in Clapham and how anyone living out in the country didn't know they were born.

"I bet hearing those old bombs going over every night really frightens you," he said. Josie didn't answer: she wouldn't tell him it did but she wouldn't lie either.

"Well, it doesn't scare me," said Tom. "They won't drop here. The Germans only set their bombs to fall on places which matter. You have to live somewhere Hitler worries about if you want to be *really* frightened. Not that I ever was."

"Then why come here?" said Josie.

"My Mum got scared. I'd have stayed. It was exciting."

Somehow, Josie didn't believe him.

"You'll never hear the doodlebug motors cut out right over your head, not like we did," Tom continued. Josie had a depressing thought. *Have I got to listen to this all the time now?*

The trouble was, the kids at school couldn't hear enough of it. Alfie Perkins seemed to think Tom was a returning war hero. Even the teacher asked him to tell the class all about what had happened. Josie could see he loved watching their faces as he described shops and houses being destroyed, people killed, and repairs made just in time for them all to be knocked down again the next night.

By the time school finished for the day, Tom seemed a person of mystery, someone with news from another world.

Many children felt quite ashamed to live in a safe place where nothing terrible ever happened.

3

The Bomb Squad

Frank Brown was not in the least ashamed about living in a place where nothing terrible ever happened. He'd had quite enough of terrible things happening. Besides, he didn't believe there was any place in the world safe from danger.

Frank was a lieutenant in an Army Bomb Disposal Unit, on a big army base near where Josie lived. Before the war he had been a watchmaker – he loved intricate, delicate parts which needed skill and patience to put together. When he joined up, he looked for a way to put his skills to good use in the war. Defusing unexploded bombs needed long hours of patience and sureness of touch. It seemed the ideal thing.

Now, three years on, he had come safely through many close encounters.

He was talking one morning to Bob Wilkins, his sergeant and, after all they'd been through together, his close and trusted friend. They were in their jeep, on their way to yet another day's training.

"Do you remember the first enemy bomb we saw?" Frank said.

"Don't I just," Bob replied. "Back in 1940, it was. When we got the call to go out after that raid on London, I tell you, my stomach turned over."

"No one who isn't in bomb disposal can know the feeling when you see the tail fins of an unexploded bomb sticking up out of the wreckage and you know that nobody's going to make it safe but you," said Frank. "But the first was the worst. Would I keep my nerve? Could I do it when it came to the push?"

"It took you four hours," said Bob. "You were running with sweat when you came out."

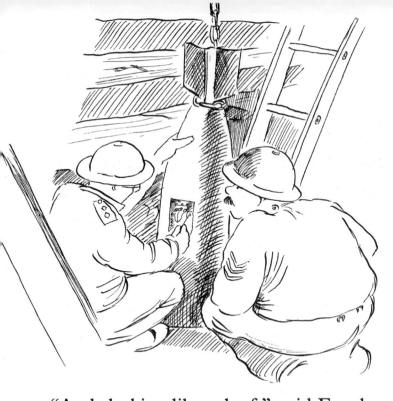

"And shaking like a leaf," said Frank.

"It didn't show," said Bob. "You did it. We knew you would."

But after that, feeling for the fuses and timers of unexploded bombs and making them safe had been Frank's job. Many of his friends had not survived. Things could go wrong. A bomb could blow up without a second's warning.

"And now come the doodlebugs," said Bob.

The doodlebugs. Frank was quiet as he thought about them. They were fired from launching sites in northern France. They flew at over 400 miles an hour, faster than any of our fighters except the new Hawker Tempest.

They were set to cut out and drop precisely when they were over London. And when they dropped, they exploded. Only now and again did one fail to go off, and then only when the timer wasn't right and the bomb fell short. Then it might stay where it landed, sticking up into the air like a dead shark.

A few weeks before, two had done just that and teams had worked for hours sorting out the horrible insides of the things, knowing that every second might be their last. Every bomb squad had been told what they found – but being told and seeing for yourself are very different indeed. And besides, the two doodlebugs were different in small but important ways.

Finally they arrived at the training ground. As they got out of the jeep Frank turned to Bob: "We'll get one of our own to sort out," he said. "You mark my words. One will fall round here and we'll be the poor twerps who'll have to deal with it. I feel it in my bones."

"Look on the bright side," said Bob. "The chances are against it. Those that aren't shot down usually explode where they land. There aren't many that don't."

"But there are a few," said Frank. "And one's going to come our way."

"You're a born pessimist," Bob replied.

"In this war, it's best," said Frank. "That way, you don't get disappointed."

4

DOODLEBUG!

It was a windy, rainy night near the end of July. Over the last few weeks the doodlebugs seemed fewer in number. Or was that just wishful thinking? Josie still couldn't lie in bed without counting them going overhead, however hard she tried.

Once one had gone, she waited holding her breath until the next. Three . . . four . . . yes, the time between them was getting longer. Here came number five. Listen to it. Just five minutes now from London, after dodging guns, fighters and balloons. Some family was very soon going to know all about this one as it reached its target and . . .

But what's happened? Where's it gone?

No. Josie couldn't believe it. *The engine roar had stopped, suddenly, without even a tiny echo, leaving an empty, silent sky. And it was directly overhead.*

There was just a little pause of a few

seconds when nobody could move or make a sound, a few seconds of the purest terror. Only one thought passed through Josie's head: *Poor Tom. He came all this way to be safe. Now look what's happening!*

There was a rending crash. Dust showered Josie as the roof shook over her head. The floor suddenly tipped like a ship at sea listing to one side when it was torpedoed. She waited, unable to breathe, for the whole cottage to collapse and bury her in bricks and wooden joists – before the blast from the flying bomb carried them all away.

One second passed. Two. Three.

She breathed again. This was amazing. There was just complete silence.

Isn't heaven quiet, she thought.

Then she realised she was moving. How could this be? It took her a moment to realise that the floor was sloping towards the wall and her bed was sliding down with her still in it.

She couldn't see anything, just a cloud of brick dust which got in her hair and eyes and made her cough. She sat up, tried to scramble out – but then the

bed stopped. It had fetched up against something hard. What was it? She reached out fearfully and touched it. Her fingers met black metal.

She took her hand away as if she was dodging the strike of a poisonous snake. *She had touched the side of the doodlebug.*

But this was a bomb? Why then hadn't it gone off like bombs were supposed to?

She heard a sound – a tiny, frightened

voice from below her. "Mummy!"

For the first time, Josie thought about what might lie outside the room. How were the rest of her family? Was anybody hurt? *Was anybody dead?*

Another voice. "Hush, David. Nasty Mr Hitler can try all he likes but I won't let him get my David." It was Mum. She shouted, "Josie. Can you hear me? Are you all right?"

Was she? Josie hadn't considered whether she might be hurt. She gave herself a quick examination. Bruised, shaken – but no more.

"Yes, Mum. I'm fine."

"Thank God for that," Mum replied.

"What about you and David?" Josie asked. All their voices sounded far away and muffled, as if they were talking through cotton wool.

"We're OK. What about Mabel?" she heard Mum worriedly ask. Josie crept over to where the voices seemed to come from. She imagined Mum sitting on her bed with David in her arms, the two of them covered in white dust and even in the darkness standing out like ghosts.

"What about Tom?" said Mum.

As if in answer came the sound of crying from where Josie's room used to be. "Oh my Lord. What are we to do?"

"Is that you, Mabel?" Mum called. "Are you and Tom all right?"

Then came another, complaining voice. "Mum, you said we'd be safe here. I thought the doodlebugs didn't drop in the country."

"It's not my fault, Tom," Josie heard Aunt Mabel answer. "I can't think of everything."

Tom suddenly shouted: *"Let me out!"*

"Shut up, Tom," hissed Mabel. "Don't show yourself up. Anyway, no one can hear you."

Yes, but Tom was right, Josie thought. How were they to manage getting out? She clambered over to the ladder which should let her climb down to join the rest. Her heart sank. The ladder was gone. The entry was blocked with bricks and wood. She was trapped up there.

"But we can't get out. Any of us," Mum called back.

Auntie Mabel seemed to have pulled herself together. "Don't worry. The good Lord will provide," she answered. "He got us through the blitz. He'll get us through this."

"He'd better," said Mum.

Josie had realised something awful. "We mustn't move," she cried. "Or we

might set it off."

"We'll have to wait," said Mum. "Someone's bound to come soon."

But it seemed hours as they waited, not daring to move – hardly even daring to breathe – before there was the sound of a car engine outside and then voices.

"Hell's teeth, look at that," said the first voice.

"Air Raid Wardens," another voice called. "Can anyone hear me?"

Mum risked a shout. "There are five of us, one's a baby. I think we're all OK."

"If that's so, then it's a miracle," said the first voice.

"Thank the Lord you've come. Please get us out," Auntie Mabel pleaded. And Tom cried with her – "Yes, get us out."

"Sorry," said one of the wardens.

"We daren't touch the place. Not with that thing there."

"We'll have to send for the bomb squad," said the other.

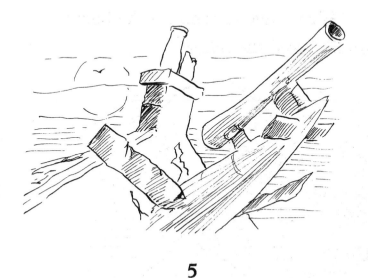

5

Dangerous work

Dawn was breaking. Wind and rain had
died away: the sky was clearing. Today
might be fine for a change. So Frank
Brown thought as the line of army trucks
climbed the hill to what was left of the
cottage. The whole team gasped together

as they saw the sight against the horizon
in the lightening sky. The doodlebug's
tail and engine pointed upwards to the
heavens like a weird statue. Its stubby
wings were broken: bits of metal and spar
mingled with bricks and wooden beams
on the ground. The bomb had not hit the
cottage directly – if it had, there would be
nobody left in it alive. The main force had

been taken by outhouses to the side of the main building, but the doodlebug had sliced through one side wall and taken floors and ceilings with it. What was left of the cottage seemed to be leaning into the ground. The bomb disposal team picked their way through coal and logs from a fuel store. And the doodlebug had not exploded. Yet.

Bomb Squad and Air Raid Wardens stood together 200 yards away. "How many in the house?" asked Frank.

"Five," said the warden. "They all sound OK."

Frank didn't wait to comment on how lucky they'd been.

"Sergeant," he called. "Here's another scary effort coming up."

"Then let's get started," Bob replied.

He at once detailed the soldiers to begin clearing the wreckage of the house and get the people out. With painstaking care they removed loose bricks and whole slabs of wall bit by bit, making sure the main stairs were safe to creep up and then down again without disturbing the delicate

mechanisms inside the
doodlebug.

At last they began to
get people out. First David,
amazingly fast asleep, then
Mum, then Tom, now fascinated
by what was going on. Last of all
came Auntie Mabel,
by this time too
shocked even to
mention that the
Lord had
provided at
last. They
were all
brought back
to where the
wardens waited.

"Josie's still in the attic," said Mum.

"Go back and get her," said Bob.

"Can't get up there, sarge," said a soldier. "Not without the whole lot coming down. That would set this thing off for sure."

Mum went pale. "But what about Josie?" she wailed. Frank made a decision. "We've got to go in and sort this blighter out first," he said. "It's Josie's best chance."

Josie could hear the scrabbling underneath her as the soldiers clawed their way through to the others. She knew someone had come to rescue them, though she had no idea

who. She waited for someone to pull the floorboards away and get her down. That seemed hours ago now. Everyone had gone away. They weren't going to

leave her there, surely?
The first feelings of panic
began to come.
Somebody *do* something,
please, she thought.

At last she heard a voice below her,
through the piles of rubble. "Josie? Are
you all right?"

"Yes."

"My name's Frank. The only way we
dare get you out is to make the bomb safe
first. Do you understand that?"

"Of course I do," Josie answered. She
felt quite indignant that he felt he need ask.

"I might be a long time. You must stay
very still."

"I will," she answered.
And she would, even
though her throat was
dry with dust and she

so badly wanted to go to the lavatory. She sat on the broken floorboards in a corner of the sloping attic, put her arms round her knees and prepared to wait.

Frank now started the work he was trained for. Every sound, every sight round him faded away. There was just him and the doodlebug in a silent struggle. And he was determined to win it.

This flying bomb contained nearly a ton of explosive. Inside there would be at least two fuses. The first was in the nose. It was a nasty one – electrical, powered by a battery and, if that failed, a little generator. He wasn't sure how either of them were connected.

But there was also a switch on the outside of the body to set the fuse off if the bomb made a belly landing. Well, this one had landed nose first, but it hadn't gone off, so perhaps neither battery nor generator were working. So if he disconnected the switch . . .

"Can you still hear me, Josie?" he softly called.

"Yes," she answered.

"I'm sorting out the first fuse now. I think I can manage it."

Josie waited. There was a scrabbling noise as if bricks were being removed, then silence. She thought she heard the snip of pliers, but she couldn't be sure. The wait seemed an eternity.

Disconnecting the switch was delicate work. First, Frank had to find it. The doodlebug's nose had burrowed into the concrete floor of the coalhouse. For a few minutes he was pulling bricks and loose bits of concrete out of the way to expose it.

There it was, along with twisted pieces of the little propeller. Inside it was a tiny electrical fuse. The trouble was, it was different from the ones he was used to. He leant forward right inside the doodlebug and shone his torch.

Yes, that must be it. A snip with the pliers here . . . and here . . . and we'll either be safe or blown off the earth into who knows where?

He waited. Nothing happened. He'd done it. Well, the first part, anyway.

"That's one done," he whispered.

"Wonderful," Josie whispered back. But she wouldn't allow herself to be hopeful yet.

Frank knew that the people who'd made these bombs weren't stupid. They knew their first fuse might not work. On top of the warhead was a mechanical fuse designed to go off on impact. This time it hadn't. He muttered a little prayer. *"Please* let this one be in a place I can reach."

Now he had to scramble over to near where the wing spar had stuck out of the body, before hitting the house had wrenched it off. He clawed his way to the body's upper surface, right over the warhead. Here was a little pocket with a bakelite cap to unscrew.

"Can you hear me still?" he called.

"Yes," Josie replied.

"I've found the second fuse," he whispered.

This was another nasty one. One mistake, the tiniest of unsteady tremors, and here would be another chance to blow them all away in a split second. He held his breath and concentrated.

"I'm doing them, Josie," he said.

Josie waited without moving.

Snip. Snip. Snip.

At last. Now what? That possible third fuse.

This could be a real killer. It was a delayed action fuse, normally set to go off after two hours. But the Germans might be able to set it to any time they liked.

This delayed action fuse – if this particular flying bomb had one – should be in a little pocket with a screw cap like the one he'd just made safe. The trouble was, where on the body might it be?

He felt all the way round as far as he could. Nothing. Above him were ceiling joists and the floorboards of the attic. He couldn't get past them without risking

blowing the whole lot up. But somewhere up there, the screw cap for the third fuse had to be. If it was there at all. Which meant . . .

His heart sank.

No, it was too much to ask. He'd be putting a ten year old girl in danger – enough to get him court-martialled.

But what else could he do? He had to know if taking the risk of shifting those floorboards and scrambling through somehow was justified.

He made his mind up. He straightened up as far as he could and called through the smashed ceiling and blocked stairway.

"Josie?"

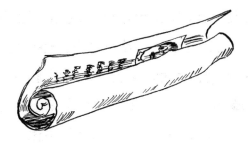

6

Josie's triumph

Josie scrambled down the sloping floor to where Frank's voice came from. "Yes?" she said.

"Josie, you've got to do something for me. I daren't try getting through to the attic because there's still a chance this

thing might blow. I think there may be just
one fuse left and once we've got that out
of the way we're safe."

"I see," said Josie. "Why are you
telling me?"

"Because you'll have to find it."

Josie said nothing for a moment.
She couldn't believe this.

Frank went on. "Josie, there may be
a little cylinder with a screw cap on
the end sticking out of the side of
the body. If there isn't, we're

OK. If there is, I've got to get through and sort it out. Can you see anything."

The morning sun filtered through cracks in the walls. By its light she looked at the blank side of the doodlebug. "No," she answered.

"Are you sure? What about the other side that you can't see?"

"I don't know." This question sounded stupid. It deserved a sarcastic answer. "I can't see it, can I?"

"Josie," said Frank quietly. "This is important."

She felt ashamed. This was no time to be funny. Everybody, she realised, was depending on her: Frank, Mum, David, Auntie Mabel, Tom – and she herself. She wanted to get out of here, didn't she?

Carefully she pulled herself up to the doodlebug's body. She felt its side where she could lean round and see it. "Nothing here," she said.

She'd have to get round further. Half the house seemed to be wedged up against the other side of the doodlebug. But she worked away busily with her fingers, dislodging bits of brick, plaster, more dust – until . . .

Yes, Frank was right. Here was the sticking-out bit, made of some sort of bakelite, and here was its screw cap.

"Got it," she said.

She could reach just enough to get her fingers round the cap. It wouldn't move.

"I can't unscrew it," she said.

"Don't even try!" said Frank urgently.

"Let me come through."

But she *was* trying, with all the strength in her fingers. And at last it moved. A little more – and a little more – and it was *off!*

"Got it," she cried triumphantly.

"Don't do any more. Wait for me," Frank called desperately.

But now Josie felt reckless. Nothing could stop her. She reached in with her fingers. Yes, she felt something.

"There's something in here," she said. "Shall I pull it out?"

"NO!" Frank was about to shout – but too late.

"I've got it," she said.

Frank waited for the blast which would hurl them off the earth.

Nothing happened.

At last he could speak. "What is it?"

Josie was staring at the object in her hands. "It's just a rolled-up piece of cardboard," she said.

Frank couldn't help what he did next. Relief hit him like a tidal wave. Suddenly it seemed almost funny. He burst into wild peals of laughter. "Is that all the Nazis could find to put in there? We really are going to win this war."

He pulled himself together. "Come on, Josie," he said. "Let's get you out of here."

★   ★   ★   ★

It seemed a long time before the soldiers cleared a way through for Josie to come outside and see the sun again. When she did, she felt a different person from the one she was when she had gone to bed the night before.

She looked at Tom. Yes, there was no mistake. He actually looked envious. *She* had the stories to tell at school now. And if Alfie Perkins ever said, "What do girls know about it?" again, she'd clock him one.

There was Frank Brown, smiling in front of her. They'd been through a lot together in the remains of the cottage and yet she'd not seen him till now.

"Josie," he said. "I want to shake you by the hand. If they ever give medals for this, I'll make sure you get one."

She glowed with pride. One day their cottage would be rebuilt. Dad would come back from sea and Uncle Bert from France with great tales of the war. Or so they hoped. But Josie wouldn't just have to sit and listen, because now she had her own tale to tell – and a roll of German cardboard to prove it.

Doodlebugs

How they started

By 1942, the Germans no longer had enough aircraft or pilots to keep up a bombing campaign. But they did have some wonderful rocket scientists, led by the famous Wernher von Braun. He was based at Peenemunde, a little village on the north-west coast of Germany. By 1943, the Allies were getting reports that a secret weapon was being developed there. Soon it was clear: the Germans had invented a flying bomb.

The doodlebugs

The Germans knew that soon D-Day would come, when the Allies would invade France. They wanted to stop it, and planned a flying bomb attack to start before the invasion. But the first flying bombs did not come over until a month after D-Day. When they came, though, the effect was awful – and it wasn't army bases and airfields that were hit, but ordinary people. The flying bombs came by both night and day, without warning, destroying whole streets with their blast. People underneath heard them flying over – but if the noise stopped overhead, then that doodlebug would fall on *you!*

Keeping the doodlebugs out

The armed forces tried to destroy the flying bombs before they reached their targets. Anti–aircraft guns were used on the coast. Bombs which got past them were attacked by Spitfires, Tempests and Mustangs, fast enough to chase and shoot them down. Sometimes the fighters came very close and tipped them over with their wings. Last of all were the barrage balloons, making a sort of net of cables which some flying bombs flew into.

The V2

The Germans called the doodlebug the V1 – the first Vengeance weapon. What followed it was even worse – the V2 – a huge rocket which could not be shot down. The end of the war was near though, and, luckily for the Allies, the V2 campaign started far too late to change the war's course. But when the war ended, the scientists at Peenemunde were captured by the Americans, and taken across the Atlantic. The Apollo missions to the moon and all the American voyages into space were masterminded by that very same Wernher von Braun, who became a US citizen and went on working as before.

Bomb Disposal

As soon as the war started, bomb disposal squads were set up in the Army, Navy and Air Force. They were never short of work: here during the Blitz, overseas defusing bombs and clearing minefields. They didn't have to clear many flying bombs – but those they did posed great problems. It's true that once, instead of a sophisticated delayed action fuse, they found some rolled-up cardboard!

It is hard and incredibly hazardous work, demanding a special sort of bravery. And of course it never stopped with the end of the war. There are still minefields, in the Falklands, Bosnia, Angola and many other places, and now there are often terrorist bombs to be dealt with. We owe the Bomb Squads a lot, and will go on doing so.

Pick up a SPARKS to read exciting tales of what life was really like for ordinary people.